Congratulations!
Marcie

For Charles, Laura and Andrea
J. McK. M.

Text Copyright © 1996 by Jean McKeon Martin
Illustrations Copyright © 1996 by Frank Stinga

Published by Longmeadow Press, 100 Phoenix Drive, Ann Arbor, MI 48104.
All rights reserved. No part of this book may be reproduced or utilized in any form or by any
means, electronic or mechanical, including photocopying, recording or by any information storage
and retrieval system without permission in writing from the Publisher. Longmeadow Press and
the colophon are registered trademarks.

Cover & interior design by Frank Stinga
ISBN: 0-681-21643-3

Printed in Singapore

First Edition
0 9 8 7 6 5 4 3 2 1

THE EMPEROR'S OLD CLOTHES

written by Jean McKeon Martin
Illustrated by Frank Stinga

Don't ever let
your bath water
scum over!

Jean McKeon Martin

LP LONGMEADOW PRESS

"I will not be made a fool of again!" screamed the Emperor. "Never again will I be tricked into parading through the kingdom without any clothes on!" The Emperor's face turned beet red and his triple chins jiggled as he screamed.

The servants huddled in the corners as the Emperor raged.

Only Loyal, the Royal Valet, was not afraid. "Your Majesty.."

"Silence!" cried the Emperor as he dressed. "I shall never remove my clothes again!"

"But, Your Majesty!"

"Quiet!" shouted the Emperor.

Loyal shrugged. The Emperor had been humiliated, but surely this was not the solution, he thought.

That night Loyal laid out the Emperor's bed clothes and prepared his bath. "Nonsense!" said the Emperor. "I will never remove my clothes. No bath!"

In the morning, the Emperor came to
breakfast rumpled and wrinkled. He did not
smell very fresh.

"Your Highness," said Loyal a few days later, "perhaps you would allow us to draw your bath and wash your garments?"

"Never!" said the Emperor.

A foul smell began to follow the Emperor everywhere. The servants complained, but none dared speak to the Emperor.

At dinner three servants fainted from the odor. Loyal helped them up before the Emperor noticed.

"Your Majesty," Loyal said, "perhaps you think it is time to bathe?"

"Silence!" cried the Emperor.

"But, Sire.."

"Silence!"

As weeks passed the odor grew more foul.
Plants wilted whenever the Emperor walked
by. Ladies of the court held perfumed cloths
to their noses and kept their distance.

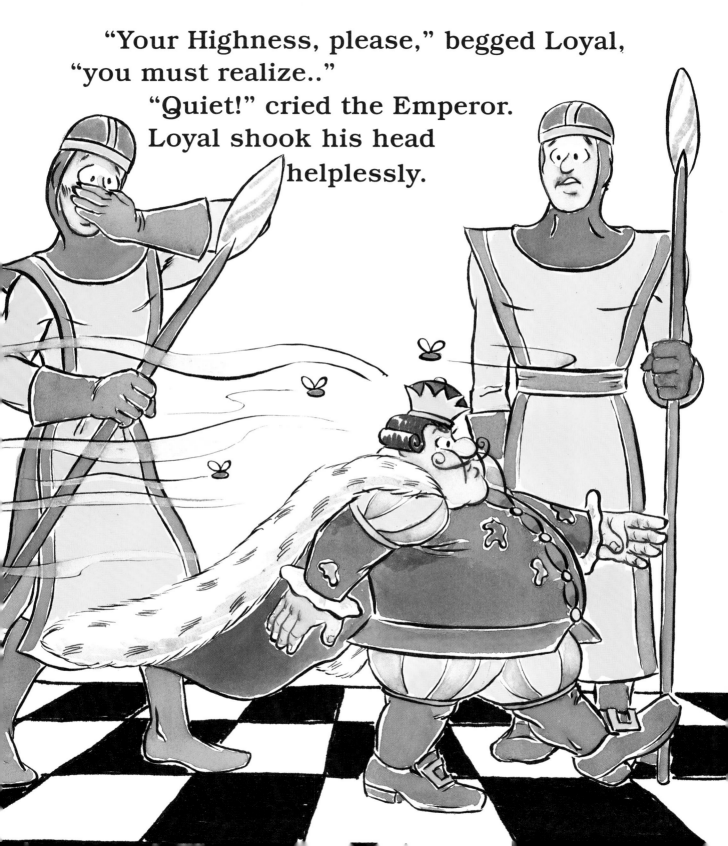

Flies soon circled the Emperor. Their constant buzzing only added to his repulsiveness.

"Perhaps it is time, Sire," said Loyal.

"Ridiculous," said the Emperor.

Loyal sighed.

"Prepare my steed," announced the Emperor. "Today I shall survey my kingdom."
When the Emperor approached, his stallion whinnied and stomped. He shook his head and snorted in disgust.

The Royal Grooms subdued him at last, and the horse reluctantly allowed the Emperor to mount. The downtrodden animal plodded through the streets, swatting flies with his tail. Loyal rode ahead of the foul display.

As they neared, shopkeepers closed their doors to shut out the stench. Babies screamed and desperate mothers shielded their children from the odor and the vile air.

The Emperor's horse pressed on. He could barely see through watery eyes and his nose burned. When he could take no more, he kicked and reared. The Emperor clung on for dear life. The stallion bolted and raced toward the woods in search of fresh air.

"Whoa!" cried the Emperor. "Whoa, I say!" The horse would not stop. The Emperor lost his grip and was thrown off deep in the woods.

Loyal found him bruised and angry.

"Fool horse!" said the Emperor. "Whatever got into him?"

"Your Majesty," said Loyal, "perhaps your clothes are...a bit ripe."

"Nonsense!" said the Emperor.

"Sire, it has been over a year.."

Loyal was interrupted by a guttural rumbling sound deep in the forest.

"What is that?" cried the Emperor.

The mournful wail grew louder and closer.

"I do not know!" Loyal said as he pulled the Emperor up alongside him. The rumbling emerged from the woods. A huge moose with flared nostrils barreled towards them.

"Hurry!" shrieked the Emperor. They galloped away and the moose lumbered after them. When he couldn't keep up, his low, plaintive bellow echoed through the forest.

The Emperor was still shaken when they reached the castle.

"Loyal, what was that all about?"

"Your Highness," said Loyal. "I believe that moose thought you were another moose."

"You jest!" said the Emperor.

"No, Sire, I do not. You have not bathed or changed your clothes in such a long time you have become quite, how shall I say it, odiferous. I am certain the moose confused your aroma with that of another moose."

"That bad?" the Emperor asked.

Loyal nodded.

"Is that what caused my horse to bolt?"

Loyal nodded.

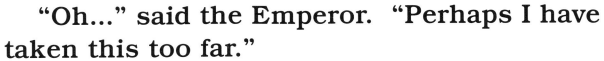

"Oh..." said the Emperor. "Perhaps I have taken this too far."

"Perhaps," agreed Loyal.

"Well, then," the Emperor commanded, "draw my bath."

"Certainly," said Loyal, "and your clothes?"

"Burn them!"

The Emperor lazed in his tub. Loyal
refilled it with clean, hot water each time
it scummed over. Hours later, the Emperor
emerged scrubbed and wrinkled.
The scent of bath oils lingered.

"Loyal, bring fresh clothes," the Emperor commanded.

The door to the Royal Garment Room held fast when Loyal tried to open it. He struggled and strained. With a final heave the door groaned open.

A cloud of plump moths billowed out and fluttered away.

Loyal gaped at the few uneaten scraps scattered on the floor. The one portly moth who remained struggled to fly.

"Your Majesty," said Loyal, "perhaps it is time to summon the tailor."